For my dad

and Tom, Chester, Blackie, Mitzi,
Bagpuss and Alfred

ORCHARD BOOKS
338 Euston Road, London NW1 3BH
Orchard Books Australia
Hachette Children's Books
Level 17/207 Kent Street, Sydney, NSW 2000

First published in Great Britain in 2006

Text and illustrations © Sam Lloyd 2006

A CIP catalogue record for this book is available from the British Library.

ISBN 1 84362 947 X

3 5 7 9 10 8 6 4 2

Printed in China

Mr Pusskins

Sam Lloyd

ORCHARD BOOKS

This is the story of a little girl called Emily, and her dear cat, Mr Pusskins.

Emily adored Mr Pusskins.

Each morning,
she would invent
fun games for
Mr Pusskins to play.

In the afternoons,
she'd brush his long
fur coat and tell him,

"Oh, Mr Pusskins, what a handsome boy you are! I **do** love you ever so much."

And each night, Emily would snuggle up in bed and read Mr Pusskins a special story.

But Mr Pusskins
never listened.

The girl's constant babbling,

"Blah~de~blah, blah, blah,"

bored his whiskers off.
He wanted more than this dull life.

He went places he **wasn't** meant to go;

did things he **wasn't** meant to do.

And even made friends with the **Pesky Cat Gang.**

But time passed, and things **changed**.
The rain fell, and an icy wind blew.

The things Mr Pusskins wasn't supposed
to do weren't fun any more. And his new
friends weren't really very nice.

How lovely it would be to
have someone to brush his fur,
and tell him how much they loved him.

He felt all **alone**.

Then down the grey streets fluttered a tatty old poster. It was a picture of Mr Pusskins!

He stared at the photo.
What a bad-tempered cat he looked.
Emily had given him **everything**
a cat could ever dream of . . .

LOST: mr Pusskins
Phone:

but he had
never been nice to her.

How
sorry
he felt.

Mr Pusskins found a phone box. He dialled the number from the poster, and waited anxiously.

Someone answered!

"Miaow," whimpered Mr Pusskins in a very sad little voice.

"Mr Pusskins! Is that you? Oh, thank goodness," said Emily. "Wait there, I'll come and get you!"

Mr Pusskins sat patiently.

Would Emily **find** him?

Did she still **love** him?

He waited
and **waited**.
But Emily didn't come.

Then, from over the mountains, he heard a car. Mr Pusskins' heart leapt!

It was Emily! His dear Emily was coming for him!

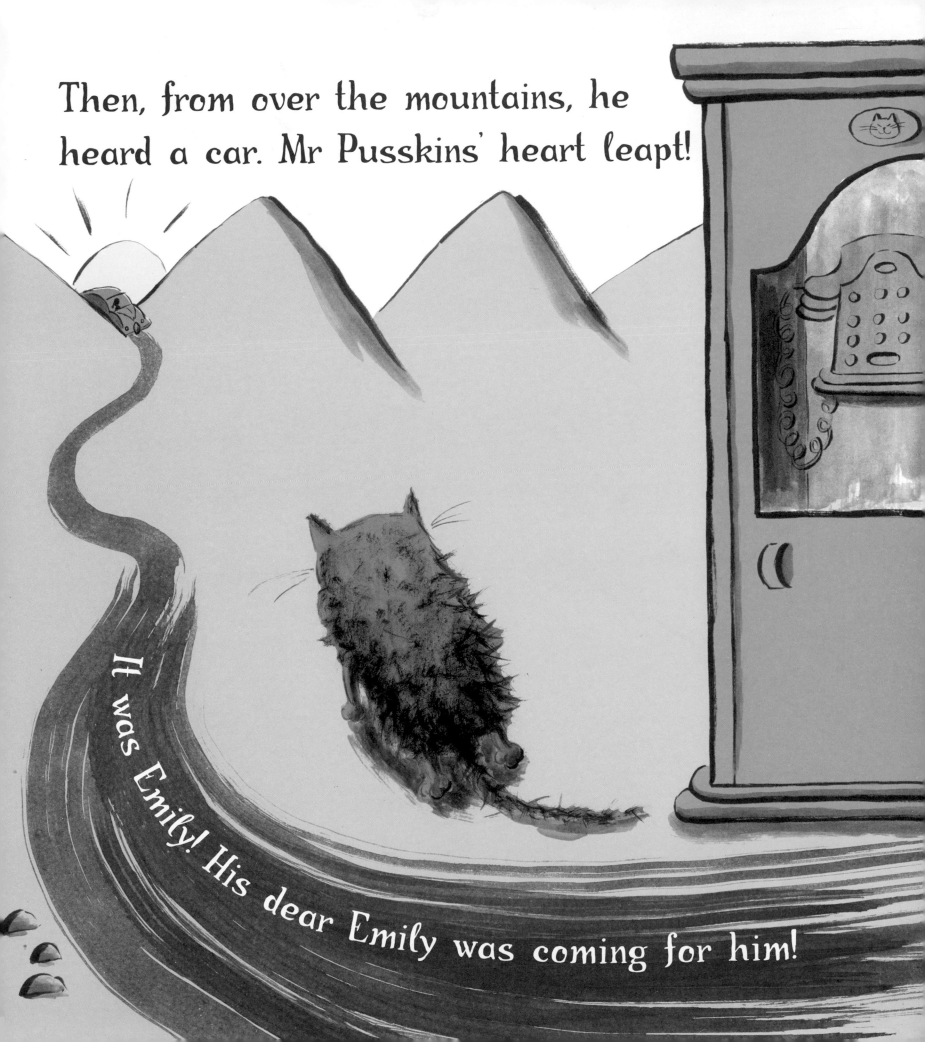

The car

got nearer

and nearer

and then . . . .

Br

... sped straight past.

"MIAAAAOOOOOOww!" wailed Mr Pusskins. "Emily doesn't love me any more."

But then . . .

rrrrrm

. . . the car screeched to a halt and Emily jumped out. "Mr Pusskins! My **beautiful** Mr Pusskins!" she cried. "I didn't recognise you!"

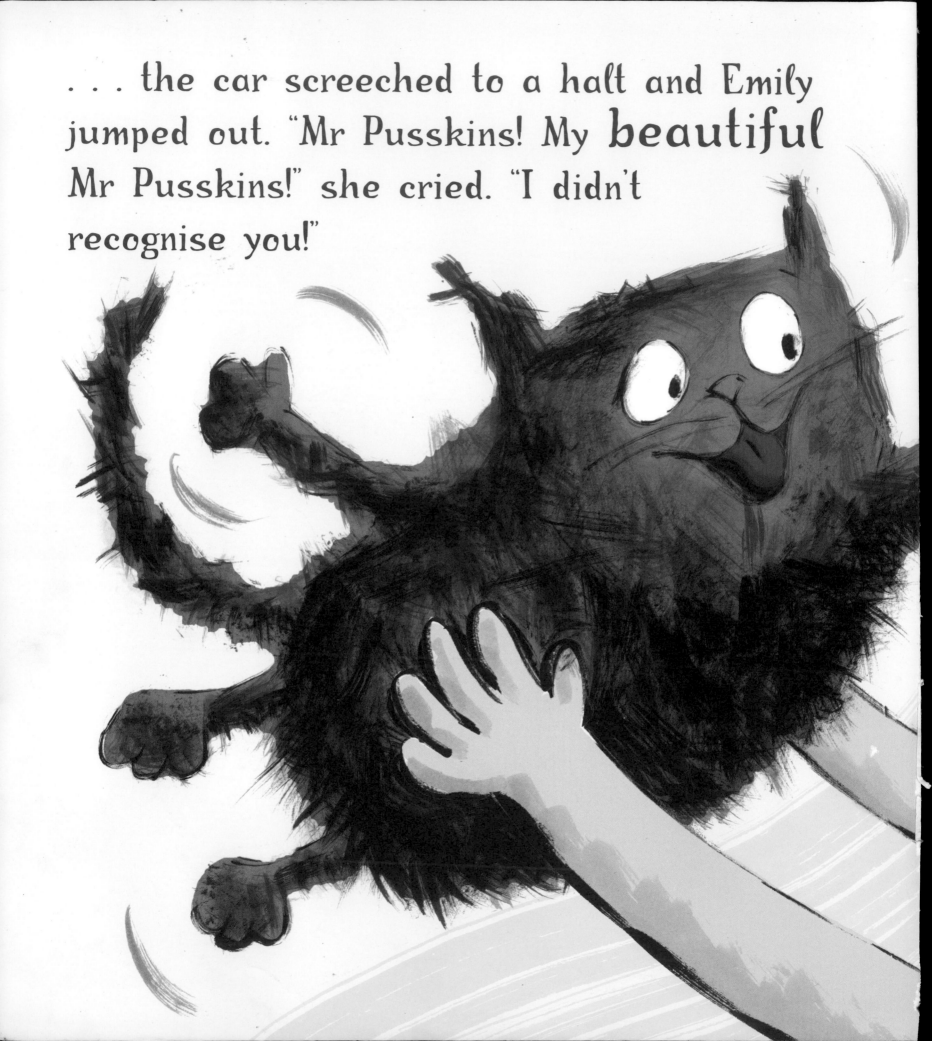

Emily scooped up her dear cat.
At last, they were

together
again!

This is the end of the story of a little girl called Emily, and her dear cat, Mr Pusskins.

Mr Pusskins **adores** Emily.

Every evening, he cuddles her and **purrs** gently while she reads to him.

And now both Emily and Mr Pusskins realise how lucky they are to have **each other**.